For the love o

by

Christopher J. F. Gibson

Dedication

This book is dedicated to all cat-lovers and especially those who

rescue cats.

Chapter 1

Clouseau demands to be noticed as no common cat since he isn't one. With a slender frame, unusually long tail and a tiny face he turns heads. He claims Burmese parentage and I think he fancies himself. When he came from the Home for Lost and Abandoned Cats he seemed really happy to change his name from Peter. From that point on, a narcissian character trait was noted in the little fella; that was, until he was "done-over" by the vet.

Clouseau stretched, as only a cat can, extending his front legs one at a time to their absolute limit while his body reached out behind him to its fullest extent. His claws bit into the hearthrug with enthusiasm as he pulled himself upright. 'Nice', he thought, 'but I could have done with a little more purchase! Another go should do it. Ahhh, just right!' With his workout complete, he marched over to me and looked me hard in the eye.

'Well, what's for supper?'

'Nothing; yet', I said without any conviction. My hesitancy was from realising that when you sleep three times a day for five hours at a time, then supper is a tri-daily event too. He never lets me forget this and I'm always reaching for the tin.

'H' hmm, if you don't mind me interrupting your daydream old chap, what's for supper?'

It has become heartless to refuse such politeness. With a bounce in his step he directs me to the kitchen and his food cupboard.

'Please, no messing about now. Really anything will do as long as it's special and very quick!'

Special meant almost anything except hard chicken-flavoured nuggets. Tins were acceptable if served with a flourish. Really special were:

Duck in sauce

Chicken fillets

Liver medallions in gravy.

'Just give me any tin' he'd sometimes say *'before I become too weak to eat it. If I could open it myself I would!'*

Didn't I know it! He succeeded once in opening the fridge and had been rewarded with five free-range eggs arriving like tiny mortars on and about him in short order.

' Strewth' he'd said, *'need to be more careful.'*

I made my usual response to him. 'Good boy Clouseau'.

I mopped them... and him... up.

'What a waste!'

I had recently read in *My Cat Monthly* that raw eggs and cats didn't mix.

'Don't you know that raw egg isn't good for little cats? Why do you think that your tinned food is sterilized?'

'Beats me!'

'Well Clouseau, it's because it finishes bugs off.'

'Well I think this is a conspiracy to stop cats like me eating when they want to. I should have food on demand; up to seven small vole-equivalents a day if I want!'

'The key word is small, Clouseau.'

'Well can I have that small, whole tin of Vole-equivalent now? Please?'

Sometimes these conversations lose me and I just give in.

'Thanks!'

My expertise with the can opener was rewarded perfunctorily. A briskly uttered '...eoww' was all I got since Clouseau was far too occupied to give me standard cat-speak. I decanted the contents into his dish, adorned with its funky cat motto.

Such pleasures are hard for cats to disguise; the tail bushes and wafts gently, the bum goes up and whiskers bristle.

'That's all?'

'You'll get fat'.

'Look who's talking, you've more jumping fat than me!'

'I'm a man.'

'You're a hypocrite'.

. Cats and humans share little common logic. Humans wash, sometimes before meals. Cats wash afterwards. Each say of the other; 'No manners!' Of course dogs don't wash at all and are despised by cats...

'Watcha' going to do today Clouseau?'

'Go out!'

'Where?'

'Outside silly.'

Outside, was the back garden, a thirty-five by thirty-foot square. There were numerous hunting and hiding places for cats among the shrubs, particularly along the back fence near the apple tree and the honeysuckle.

Clouseau lives in a suburb to the South West of Glasgow, high up on the edge of the Ayrshire moorland. Wind arrives virtually unhindered from the Irish Sea. In an attempt to shelter the garden I built a stone wall on the Western side, it marking the boundary with my neighbour. Here too is my Kilmarnock willow tree which acts as a marker-post for Clouseau. It plays a significant role in his outdoor routine. A summerhouse in the far corner, doubles as a greenhouse and guestroom for stray cats and insects. The garden and its creatures pull Clouseau like a magnet.

'Hurry, hurry, there's an imposter!'

'I can't see anything.'

'Yes there is! Look!'

I looked properly and saw Biscuit, a recent incomer to the area spraying the honeysuckle. Biscuit didn't forget Clouseau's first strike and took off rather inelegantly, perhaps amazing himself by clearing the wall by two feet. Clouseau looking smug and excited by his prowess, went for a pee. To give himself just a shade more satisfaction he did it where Biscuit had been sitting. A jackdaw sitting on the summerhouse was out of his reach but he had a chatter at it anyway as he sharpened his claws on the willow tree. This was shear bravado on his part since the Jackdaw was at least his size and much meaner. To get to the summerhouse Clouseau had to cross the green stuff humans call grass. There was one thing Clouseau didn't like about this manoeuvre. He was realistic about this since the grass spends half the year under water and as a kitten had leapt into a puddle there that had been as deep as his little legs were high.

'I nearly drowned', he told any who would listen. *'I spent ages searching the horizon and the waves were this high and things lurked under the surface and bit at my toes!'* Yes, Clouseau loved an audience and like all good yarns, I suspect it became more dramatic each time he told it. *'I was marooned..!'*

He was ambivalent about the grass. He walked on it as a man not wanting to leave his footprints on the sand. His paws became light as a feather and he looked as if he could have been walking on nails.

'If I could get on the roof, I'd ...I'd..,' he faltered, as the jackdaw made a fly past along the garden wall. He flattened his back along the ground and made a Commando-style shuffle to the apple tree that provided adequate cover for surprise ambush on smaller birds. Under the apple tree was one of his favourite haunts. From there, his whole kingdom spread out in front of him. On summer evenings it was from this spot that crane-flies received serious punishment. His most trying adversaries however were Snoopy and Tara, the dogs next door. Snoopy, aptly named, was a black Collie. He was a nosey mutt with a large woolly bone who lolled about since he'd been given early retirement from the Police a year before. Sniffing at the airport had been exchanged for sniffing at bins. Tara, a black Labrador, was docile, overweight and overly-friendly. Clouseau found these traits in different ways challenging. Docility he just could not understand. Overweight, he wasn't, but not for want of trying. Over-friendliness; well that depended on what was on the menu.

Neither Tara nor Snoopy could quite figure out Clouseau. Their first encounter with him had been earlier last year. He had been snoozing under the apple tree when his reverie had been interrupted by the appalling scent of hot dog. To his sensitive nostrils they were 'high.' Cats would never allow themselves to get into a state like that.

He did however achieve a calm psyche by visualising a packet of Tasty Topping (with giblet bits) just at paws length; he then flexed his paws one at a time imagining them luxuriously teasing loops of wool from a rug. Then a wet nose poked through the fence. Clouseau gave it a quick one-two with his claws and beat a hasty retreat to his kitchen.

He oozed satisfaction as he skilfully licked between his paws.

Chapter 2.

The Vets, a small animal practice about three miles away from our house was a large old house staffed by three small vets: Carol, Carol and Caroline. Each had committed themselves to caring for small creatures' needs and exuded enthusiasm for their charges.

The Vets is an imposing building. Built of sandstone it is square and solid. Inside the vestibule a number of solid oak doors confront you. Reception is staffed by a poodle, a gushing receptionist called Rachael and a goldfish called Charlie. Charlie guards the doggie-and-cat treats, and Rachael guards the electronic till. Charlie and Rachael flirt unashamedly with the clients at the moment when they have to reach deep into their pockets for their credit cards. Charlie blows magnified kisses through the curve of his bowl.

'Hi Rachael, just calling in to make an appointment for Clouseau.'

'Oh, darling, hello; it's Clouseau Gibson, isn't it?'

'Yes, it's for Clouseau Gibson' I said quietly.

'Goody-good!' Rachael boomed. 'Clouseau Gibson is coming in for his flea-thingy, is he?'

I'm sure I saw two ferrets and a hamster scuttle off to a dark place.

'Yes" I said quietly, 'and to have his booster.'

'Oh jolly jolly good' boomed Rachael, giving me an enormous toothy grin, 'Ten-o'clock next Tuesday, and it's with Carol.'

'Which Carol? 'I enquired, since the previous visit had ended with the very very small Carol reaching for Band-Aids after Clouseau ambushed her right-hand.

'Oh... let's see now' she exclaimed loudly enough to be heard through the oak-panelled doors.

'The other Carol.'

'Other..... than, the Carol I saw last time?'

'Yes, she wasn't used to Clouseau was she?'

I thought, as I left, that smallest Carol was probably used to lacerations, but with Clouseau you really had to be decisive since he wasn't averse to expressing his disgust when he was tampered with. I thought I'd better tell him about his appointment. It would give him time to get used to the idea. Back home I unlocked the door and listened. A patter of paws raced down the stairs to meet me. I shouted 'Clouseau, I'm home!'

There returned his usual response from inside.

'Marrow...'

'Hello, fella!'

His paws curled around the door and pulled it wide open; he's surprisingly strong. With one look, just to be doubly-sure it really was me and not an imposter who might steal his grub, he led me to the kitchen, stopping on the way for a customary flop-over and tummy-tickle on the rug. I've discovered that rituals mean a lot to him. It just didn't seem fair, to tell him of the impending visit to the vets whilst he was so obviously enjoying himself.

The following Tuesday he examined the locks on his cat-transporter.

'Treachery!'

'Help!'

'Never!'

This moderated, for a while to

'Pleeese?'

'Trapped!'

'Bother, bother, bother!'

Quiet resignation is not Clouseau's style. I was trying hard to keep out of eye-contact so that he wouldn't hold being forcibly incarcerated against me too personally.

He had cautiously approached the slivers of home-cooked chicken that had been laid temptingly at the transporters entrance. I had, with a practiced push, propelled him inside. The firm approach was the only way. You have to be hard in these situations and I don't know which of us was more distressed as we had entered the Vets.

'Hello Clouie, aren't you just goooorgeous?' piped Rachael. Simultaneously, Clouseau was thinking that she was fat, and that he wasn't going to be taken-in by any female with all *her* bits still, so obviously intact.

'Save your smooch for dumb animals,' he muttered darkly.

I looked about, picking a chair between a sweet Persian cat and a white mouse absorbed with a wheel. Clouseau was in a total huff and didn't speak to anyone. It was certainly beneath his dignity to acknowledge the mouse. It, like dogs, was vermin. The Persian spoke a different dialect anyway and had a face that looked as if it had recently had a close-encounter with a spade.

He sulked.

We'd only waited five minutes when a real rumpus started. A man with a ferret had been talking to a woman in a fur coat. She had a shiatsu in her arms. Whether the ferret and taken a dislike to the dog or indeed he was avenging all mink, foxes and rabbits the world over who provide humans with warm clothing, is unclear but it broke free from its cardboard container and struck out hard, teeth bared. I think it is likely that the woman's collar resembled another ferret. Either way the ferret went for it. The woman released her grip on the dog as the ferret locked onto the collar. It killed the collar stone dead. The dog, now released from its embrace saw an opportunity to defect and deftly side-stepped a collie with its leg in plaster. It made a bolt to the open door. Here we lost sight of it. Our attentions were redirected to the woman, who, in hysterical gyrations was trying to remove the coat and its new lodger. She screamed and a parrot mimicked her. The collie suffered another minor fracture as Rachel fell over it and landed heavily.

Clouseau still sulked.

All this sort of thing was well beneath him and he feigned disinterest. I knew that one ear listened and should anyone have come near he would have reacted with lightning speed to inflict a scratch but to the casual observer he was sleeping through it all.

Caroline came in to see what was happening and retreated as the women flew past her tumbling the Guide Dog for the Blind plastic dog effigy. It rattled pathetically as it tumbled over and spilled a few coins and three washers on to the floor from its broken tail.

Carol stormed in as Rachel was rearranging her bits.

'What on earth?'

'Oh God', blurted Rachel, 'I'm so, so sorry, I should have... but it just took off and attacked her coat.' The woman's coat was, by then, on the floor, still with its new owner shaking it violently. The woman was being comforted by the woman with the white mouse.

'My Toby, he'll never find his way back', she wailed. 'And it's all his fault!'

She pointed a fat finger at the man who had, till recently, been custodian of the ferret.

'It's not my fault Mrs', he said thickly,' if you ain't got more sense than to come down here all la-di-da in a fur coat. Insensitive I'd call it, with all these animals and that.'

'How could you!' she remonstrated. 'Just get that *thing* off my coat!"

'It'll bring the collar wi' it if I do.'

The woman's face changed colour.

'What's it to be missus? Seems to me like you'd better get the dog first before it gets itself into bovver'.

'My Toby, my darling; where are you pet?' she wailed. She tottered through the door. The Collie gave a whimper as it narrowly avoided high-heel induced concussion. The fur coat looked rather sorry for itself, but its new occupant didn't seem to mind. A veneer of order returned little by little. Clouseau stirred in his transporter. There was little point in his pretending to be asleep any longer.

'Well let's have a look at you then!'

'I don't think is too pleased about this Carol'.

Clouseau pressed himself hard against the floor ears flattened out sideways. This was just in case Carol tried to bite them in the scrap he anticipated. I try, as in all these encounters, to adopt a similar low profile. I thought it best not to say too much in case Clouseau associated my voice with the injustices to be done to him. First he had to have his nails clipped, then his flea drops put on his neck and be weighed. I think he thought he wouldn't be discovered if he lay low, but Carol had already snapped off the cat carrier clasps and lifted him firmly on to the scales. She typed on the computer, the other hand still holding the scruff of his neck.

'Get off, you're making a big mistake!'

'.... now converted to Kilograms.....', Carol muttered '.....now let's see these paws fella.'

Clouseau bit, he scratched, and he summoned all the oaths in his vocabulary, yet he was still in her grasp. Then, in a flash of inspiration he went into reverse. She didn't expect that. The shelving in the office was Meccano-style and self-supporting. It contained five shelves of prescription veterinary drugs and a minor collection of leaflets. As he streaked between shelves three and four, the shelving wobbled and tumbled forward. Clouseau hung on bravely as it came crashing down heavily scattering jars, files and tubs. A kaleidoscope of tablets and liquids floated across the floor.

After the fiasco in the waiting room of which he'd been a passive observer, it now seemed as if he'd stolen at least part of the action.

The incident didn't leave him wholly unscathed. An advert for flea repellent formed a tent over his back and his tail swished and violently through the dog conditioning cream.

Our rearranged appointment was made with tight lips by Rachel. It would be in two weeks she informed me and would I 'pleeese' try and do the fleay-thingy before we came. Their insurance would cover the rest, and my credit card was only stung for twenty-seven pounds for the consultation. I imagined being assaulted by a sea of reporters with flashing bulbs igniting as we left, Clouseau's head covered by a sheet, his outstretched paw brushing aside questions with a 'No comment!' Instead, we both breathed in the cool spring air and congratulated each other on our cool dignity in the face of adversity.

'Well', he exclaimed, as the Vets disappeared from the rear-view mirror, 'some set-up that, they couldn't organize a cats dinner party in a chicken and jelly factory!'

'My feelings exactly Clouseau.'

We decided to take the scenic route home via some reservoirs. He'd been this way once before and I thought it might cheer him up to have a natter at the assorted bird-life loafing about the reservoir. He perked up as we spotted the first coot. I stopped the car by an embankment and since I had little to do for the rest of the morning, thought I'd sit and admire the view. To the South ran the moors, to the West, Paisley and five miles to the North, Glasgow's sprawling metropolis. His face pressed hard at the window of his transporter begging for freedom. He issued a stream of invitations to the birds to join him but none took up his offer. He could hardly have pleaded any louder but the window muted his attempts to persuade them. Eventually I took pity, opened the door of his carrier and hauled him over my shoulder as I have done since he was six months old. His two front paws dug in tight to my shoulder blade, his neck brushed my left ear and his back paws were planted securely in the crook of my arm. In this position he felt secure and unassailable and it gave him a jolly sight better view. I felt his claws tighten hard against my shoulder; he wouldn't have jumped, but he postured and posed as a flight of Mallards made a lazy and unstructured landing about 50 metres away. Some overturned and three of four came in too sharply and went unexpectedly underwater. Clouseau wiggled a bit and I adjusted his posture to give himself a better view of their Green Crowns sparkling against the water. Glints of sunlight refracted and danced in all directions. Clouseau squinted hard and maybe imagined he saw a plump mouse shivering on a lake of jelly.

Chapter 3

I am led to understand that as a kitten Clouseau was confined to a single room in a Paisley flat. Now he was a worldly-wise observer and occasional outdoor explorer. Travelling in the car, he approached with mixed emotions, glad to be out of the house and yet frustrated by the constraints of the vehicle and especially the carrier when he was pressed to stay in it. He probably is one of the most seasoned cat-travellers in Scotland having journeyed to the Lake District on weekend visits to my Dads once a week for eighteen months. I think that the car alternated in his regard from a terrible ogre to an object of mild curiosity. It most certainly had an intriguing smell. Strong smells and the heady combination of rubber, oil and cigarette smoke probably left his senses reeling. On the rare occasions he escaped over the garden gate he would usually be found skulking about under the chassis of the car or sitting proud as punch on the roof where he surveyed the comings and goings of visitors. He positively exuded pride as he sat bolt upright, whiskers forward and bristling, interpreting every draft of breeze.

A year prior to the Vet visit Diane and I had made contact with an organisation that re-homed cats. We had wanted a cat in our family for ages then and sought out this rescue centre. It was run by Sheila and Fiona.

'Hello Sheila, it's Chris, I was given your name by a lady called Helen.'

'Hello?'

She's deaf I thought.

'Yes, my name is Chris and...' I shouted.

'I'm not deaf dear...'

'I'm sorry.'

'Yes, it's just that Susie pulled the phone and flex around her tail and the phone fell on the floor...'

'Oh, I see,' I said, not seeing.

'And Jack has the Sellotape.'

I was being drawn in. 'Sorry?' I said.

'Well dear, it's stuck to the writing pad'.

I waited, hoping for clarification.

'So I can't write your details down.'

The penny dropped.

'I see', I said, seeing clearly this time.

'Have you got it now?' I inquired.

'Of course!'

'O.K. well it's Chris on 0141-1234567' I said, heavily emphasizing the numbers. 'Helen gave me your number.'

'She phoned me, and told me; I've got your name and number on a pad here; somewhere.'

'I just gave it to you.'

'Did you? Oh so you did.'

I was really glad that all that was settled as I didn't feel up to starting all over again.

'Chris; yes, you're the fellow who's looking for a cat.'

'Preferably a very young one Sheila.'

'The trouble is", she said, 'everyone wants a kitten but I've got a nice mother and daughter who need to be homed together.'

'I don't think I could take two', I said.

'Oh, I didn't mean that', she said, 'I was just mentioning it.'

I was forming the impression that Sheila was not going to be the easiest person to deal with.

'Just hold on dear', she said.

I held on for a few minutes. Nothing. A few more minutes elapsed. Nothing. Then faintly I heard, '...come on darlings, don't push, there is enough for everyone!'

I began to wish for some soothing computer- generated polyphonic jingle, even Greensleeves on a closed loop. Instead, I was cut-off. There was nothing for it; I dialled again. It was engaged.

'Please hold the line, the number you are calling knows you are waiting.' Then;

'Hello?'

'Hi, it's Chris again.'

'I'm so sorry, one of the cat's got trapped under the wheelchair after I'd fed them.'

That's where she'd gone; to feed the cats. Then the picture formed in my mind; a wheelchair; the delay; it made sense. Why she'd chosen to feed them whilst on the telephone to me was a mystery.

'I had to feed them then because it was 12 o'clock', she said.

'Of course', I said.

'And they go crazy when the clock strikes.'

I imagined the poor woman being overrun by a herd of cats at the chime of every hour.

'They seem to know you see', she continued.

It was a difficult to restrain my laughter as she continued her tale.

'...when it's lunchtime; they are creatures of habit you know, so when I give you Fiona's number you must reassure her that you'll be meticulous with the feeding.'

I reassured her that indeed, being a creature of habit myself, but I would attend to that necessity well.

With that she gave me Fiona's number.

I dialled Fiona's telephone number and hoped that she was more comprehensible than her friend.

Fiona spoke softly and smoothly.

'Hello?'

'Hello, Sheila gave me your telephone number to enquire about adopting a rescue cat.'

'Indeed' Fiona purred. I will give you my address. Come and see me.'

After driving three miles I found Fiona's house. I knocked.

A throaty 'woof' answered, and became a whimper as the dog realised I posed no threat. I was probably another misguided human being in search of a cat. At least it would be one less to concern himself with. I looked through the porch-door at a handsome German Shepherd with creased brown eyes. The tail thumped and as Fiona opened the door the tail beat me into submission and I hoped the rest of him was going to be as friendly.

'Meet Josh,' she said.

'Hi fella!' I said unsurely.

'Don't worry about him, he's just a softy.'

I was taken, the dog riding shot-gun, to the back of the dilapidated cottage where neat rows of centrally-heated sheds housed the feline residents. Here Fiona explained the nature of her work and I became convinced of her absolute devotion. She was certainly no ordinary

cat-lover. As we passed each of the pens she gave a quiet

resume of the characters inside, their veterinary history and their

natures. Here, an orphaned kitten, there, a pregnant mother-to-be.

"So I'll just leave you with them and you can let me know when

you've been chosen."

I was to discover how right she was! She and the dog disappeared into

the cottage. There was no choice. As I'd followed her around most of

the cats seemed to be asleep. Only one had jumped tail up

from his bunk and stretched a paw inviting me to reciprocate.

I'd turned round to greet him.

"Hello, little one!" I'd said.

Still dabbing at my hand, he welcomed me into his den.

I knelt and he hopped into the crook of my arm.

"Well chap, you're inquisitive!"

His silver-and-white coat rippled appreciatively and a

purring motor turned over inside him.

He had apparently come from a flat in the city with some

excuse attached about a child with asthma. Fiona had, of course, taken

him in.

"You deserve better". I said it quietly, so as not to startle him.

His ears twitched in appreciation.

"How do you fancy getting out of here?"

His motor changed gear and I took that as an emphatic

'Yes!! Please!!'

Turquoise green eyes looked up at me and that clinched it.

Chapter 4

It took some time to adjust to being a lodger in my own

house. I had to remember to tidy up clothes or else they had

been rearranged for me by the time I got home. I had to ensure

that I washed the cereal bowl or it was licked spotlessly clean!

I made ingenious adjustments to my routine to allow for several meal-

times. It made for an interesting jigsaw. A fleecy

hammock was constructed complete with a scratching post

and I became used to finding him napping on my desk amid a muddle of

papers. I settled into my new routine and he confided in me that he was

very glad I'd adjusted so well. He showed me how to open various

cupboards to see what they contained. He spent hours

practicing on the fridge until it yielded to his ingenuity.

A deft flick of the claw at the bottom of the door usually won

the day. Relentless paddling on the microwave lever also

produced satisfactory results. His patience was remarkable.

I attributed it to the hours he spent, ears cocked forward, trying

to out-stare some unfortunate insect which had strayed onto

the carpet. He advised me man-to-man that brilliant

manoeuvres, entertaining and remarkable though they could be, never could achieve the same result as dedicated attrition.

I learned from him; I was a willing student.

I had no idea how much one could learn from cats. My first lesson was how to be a Lazy Introspective Egotist by:

a. advanced contemplation

b. sleeping-in

c. self-admiration

The winter had been mild, so although Clouseau had experienced frost, he was surprised one morning to see a steadily falling blanket of snow.

'Quick!! Come here!!'

I was being dabbed on my chin by a damp paw.

"What is it?"

I looked at my clock and it was six o'clock (in the morning).

'There are millions of things falling out of the sky.'

He was obviously agitated since he bounced back to the window to investigate. The diffuse brightness confirmed my guess.

'It's snow', I said, 'frozen-water.'

'So it shivers?'

'No, not exactly. It's like flakes.'

'*Dandruff?*'

'No, but cold dandruff; tell you what, why don't you go and see?'

'*Not sure.*'

'Wus!'

'*O.k. O.k., but only if you come too.*'

We opened the back door and a foot of snow that had drifted against it slithered onto the lino. He looked nervously round at me.

'*It got in! Quick! Run!*'

'Don't be silly', I said, 'it's only dangerous when it's in the air.'

He took me at my word and cautiously dabbed the wet pile.

'*Seems safe to me.*'

Then in a joyous bound he leaped out of the door and snow-ploughed up to his armpits.

'*Come on in, it's great*'.

It turned out to be the heaviest snowfall for years and for forty-eight hours even to get out of the driveway would have been impossible. Cars were abandoned at grotesque angles down the road and wind piled the snow in drifts at the back of the house and muffled sounds. The temperature

wasn't too low; now and then a muffled crunch could be

heard as a mini-avalanche slid off the roof and thumped the

patio. White and soft, the layers built, subtly turning distinguishable

objects into surreal shapes. A baby-elephant raised his tusks

proudly as he gave his plant pots a ride. The branches of trees

made slippery cradles for their weighty burden. This transformation

was only slightly less remarkable than Clouseau's enjoyment.

Normally, he approached all things new with great caution.

I ventured out after him, carefully picking my steps to avoid an influx of wet snow into my boots. He meanwhile was in his element. I'd

read somewhere that cats' paws were not very sensitive to cold or heat.

Ice graced the birdbath and defying gravity he gently lifted

himself up on his back legs, paws outstretched in order to touch it.

He licked, sniffed and nibbled. It didn't bite back so it was most

probably friendly. He sat on it just in case it tried to get away.

An hour later with a frozen bum he looked at the ice

accusingly. What he accused it of I never quite found out as at

that moment a second mini-avalanche descended with a woosh.

The shock of the deluge made him sit very still.

The ice obviously had allies. They weren't friendly, in fact

they were positively dangerous. He made a strategic manoeuvre and

astounded me by leaping backward and upwards, tail erect

and fluffed out like a gigantic pipe cleaner. With front paws spread wide

he cleared the patio wall as a pole-vaulter would the high-bar and

with a tuck of his stomach, made it in one piece onto the willow

tree. Not all of him appeared to arrive at the same time and as the

willow felt the tremble it gave up its white burden.

Clouseau, trying to gain purchase, flayed panic-stricken among

the trailing branches. It was just all too much. His bottle now gone

he bit blindly at the tree and with the bark stripping above him, was

inelegantly lowered into an enveloping drift.

Two periscope ears appeared and a pink nose sneezed. Inch-by-inch appeared one very wet and frosted white cat.

'*Ashrroww!*'

We huddled by the stove and dried off together.

'*You could have warned me!*'

'I never said winter was all snow-mice and sledging' I replied, my boots encircled by an expanding puddle.

'*Aseww!*' He'd started an epidemic of sneezing.

'*What was it?*'

I repeated my earlier caution that flying ice was the most dangerous.

'*It came out of nowhere!*'

'Not exactly; it was lying in wait on the roof. I didn't see it either.'

In the spring he gave the roof maximum surveillance. For many weeks when leaving the back door, he would nervously spit in its direction ... just in case...

For now, the steam rose slowly from wet fur and knobbled socks. It was difficult not to feel sorry for him. I'm glad it was only he who observed his sodden guardian; neither of us were a pretty sight. A trickle of super-cool water etched its way down my back and it's signature onto my face.

'*Wus!*' he muttered.

Two warm towels were procured and I heated a pan of milk.

'*Can I have a drop of sherry in my milk?*'

'No'.

'*More milk then. Maybe a bit warmer this time?*'

'You're spoilt!'

'*Yes, isn't it nice?*'

My wife Dianna spoils me with her stir-fries and fillet steak and I hope that I show the same enthusiasm as he does when food is in the offing.

The snow continued to fall, and I had the luxury of telephoning my work, savouring the certainty of not making it in. Living high on the edge of the moors has many advantages. A day or two curled up with a book was a treat. He, meanwhile, found my presence mildly irritating. He was settled into a routine and I was upsetting it.

'*Are you dogging it?*'

'Yep!' I said, 'I'd wanted to see what it's like being a cat.'

'*Oh, it's nothing special but the work I have to do would quite stagger you.*'

'Really?' I replied sarcastically. 'So what do *you* do after breakfast?'

'Natter'.

'Natter at what?'

'Big black mice, especially the ones who sit on lampposts.'

'What?' I said incredulous.

'Well it takes ages to get them to fly away.'

'Oh', I said, incredulous. 'Is that it for the day?'

'Course not! There are beds to be slept on; it's not easy
for me you know, there's so many choices to make.'

'Is that it?' I enquired.

'Well, I have a quick check about to make sure
there are no intruders; then there's the snacks, we can't forget
them can we?'

'No, *you* can't!'

Sarcasm is always lost on him and in fairness he doesn't
lounge about half as much as other cats. "Patch", my Father's cat,
appears to sleep eighteen hours a day. Possibly in case he gets tired. He's
kind to himself that way and has informed Ron of the need to 'sleep-off
sleeping' in case it got the better of you.

'Then', Clouseau added, nearly forgetting, 'there's the auditing
to be done.'

This, I admit, is a truly fascinating process for those lucky enough to observe Clouseau closely. His audits are meticulous. Indoors it comprises a full reconnaissance of *all* household items. All ornaments in place? -check; piano and stool (or similar things) in position for jumping thereon? -check; food and water bowls correctly arranged? - check; sniff-mats making sure scents co-ordinate,-check; examine corners of all soft-furnishings and apply paw-stamps,-check.....etc. etc. etc.

I must give Clouseau his due, he is thorough. For him all this comes prior to his re-cataloguing of things in the garden each day.

No wonder he slept a bit later on, who could blame him? Mere humans just have to find the house keys and off they go. It wasn't easy, he reminded me again.

So for two whole days I had the fortune to observe this routine at close quarters. It was clear my presence distracted him even though I was only reading, smoking and drinking coffee. For a start I subtly distorted the everyday smells and I kept moving things so he had to start all over again. The bonus for him was the rapid responses I made to his pleas of hunger. We watched some programmes on the T.V. and he called cartoon cat Tom a 'Wuz.' He felt that Jerry should have been a cat and that Tom needed to learn to be more subtle. That was the way to catch mice, not with all that heavy-handed stuff! Golf, from Florida was *very* good fun. However, many times the men in silly checked trousers whacked the white mice, they popped up out of their burrows for more punishment. Now that's what he called sporty mice! None of this cowering behind skirting boards for hours like you got at home. These American Mice certainly had guts! Occasionally one of the men would pick up a mouse, examine it to make sure it had plenty of fight left, and pop it back down again. The mice usually sat quite still. Just occasionally, one would try to slope off and had to be brought back and be reprimanded. He'd seen some go and hide and lie shivering in the sand-dunes. They were then subjected to a lot of exotic language and attacked with a stick. It was a hard life for them on the golf course. They usually got a bit of a rest when their tormentors headed for the nineteenth hole. They could then be seen sharing their experiences while furtively nestling in a leather bag outside.

Unfortunately for escapees the unemployed and school-boys would earn extra cash by selling bags of them by the first tee.

After T.V. viewing there was a short window for sleep, an opportunity which Clouseau embraced wholeheartedly.

If nothing had caught his interest on T.V. he would make a spirited dash about the living- room followed by a significantly long rest period. Since I was at home, I cannot know if his behaviour was typical.

Two hours later however, on this snowy day, he was draped over the back of the settee snoring. I attempted to synchronise with his rhythm and have eighty-winks too!

Later, it snowed even more and the shrubs virtually disappeared in the back garden. The neighbours dug about in garages for boots and sledges and dressed in colours that should not be seen together in polite company.

'It's in case they get lost', Clouseau explained.

'It's because they haven't the sense to stay indoors!' I retaliated. Big men in tiny pom-pom hats could be seen dragging small children on enormous sledges, looking heartily fed-up with the whole retched business.

'Give me the M8 any day!' I heard one of them shout to another chap. A Scottie dog called Hamish from across the road, appeared in a reflective yellow jacket and a fluorescent extension lead before disappearing totally in a snowdrift. His owner kept a determined hold, dragging him backwards and upside-down in the direction of the front door. The owner was bitten on the ankle as a token of Hamish's displeasure.

'Honestly!' said Clouseau, *'How utterly undignified dogs can be!'*

We saw Hamish yelping and struggling as he was huckled indoors to have his vest changed.

'Yuck!!!' said Clouseau. 'It's Campbell tartan too!'

Hamish reappeared, now slavering at the dining-room window.

'Don't ever dress me up like that Dogs' Dinner!'

I imagined Hamish daydreaming of looking in a mirror and seeing a tartan waistcoat with a diamante epaulets adorning his shoulders; a yellow collar and ankle chains.

Hamish didn't reappear but Clouseau kept a watch 'just in case...'

I think he was looking for an opportunity to snigger. He groomed his silky coat with pride. He felt swell. A quick manicure now and he'd earned a nibble or two of something nice.

As I made tea he sat on the bench beside me and gave helpful advice on preparation.

'Too much salt!.. I don't like it!'

"This is for me," I replied.

'Still too much; it's bad for you, and anyway you might give me the left-overs.'

'Unlikely!'

I scraped the salt off the top of the chicken anyway.

'More garlic!'

'What?'

'More garlic!'

'Why?'

'You like it!'

'So do you!'

'Touch of herbs'.

I added the herbs.

The chicken breast was divided equally, one large bit for me,
one small bit for him. As I turned to the sink to drain the vegetables
I caught him licking my plate.

I enjoyed my piece of chicken and he remarked that it was
quite alright, but next time would I please add tomato sauce.
By then I was ready to agree to anything.

'Sit on the sofa!' I said.

\

'Don't patronise me; dogs sit, cats lounge!'

Whilst he lounged, I ate my pudding. I was not however encouraged
to lounge after *my* meal.

'Yow; now please?'

'Five minutes Clouseau!'

'Yow, now, pleeeeeease!'

Yow is a sticky green present decoration made of shiny ribbon,
rather like a small rosette. At Christmas my dad had tied

a piece of string to it and made what transpired to be the best cat toy ever invented. The string had been chewed, licked, tormented and knotted. The sticky green decoration now much stickier than before. Yow lives in the kitchen drawer. He was in residence this evening and since I wasn't going anywhere, I was happy for him to spend sometime in Clouseau's company. He probably wasn't, as he usually got a good duffing-up before I called " Time!"

I never left him alone with Clouseau since he had a sneaky trick of wrapping himself around his tummy and ears simultaneously and then tormenting him rotten. Wherever Clouseau hid, he seemed to get there, if not first, then at the same time.

Clouseau was mightily chuffed when he caught Yow unawares and would proudly pick him up, head thrown back and deliver him to either me, Dianna or his basket depending on just how magnanimous he felt.

As I opened the kitchen drawer, I let Clouseau savour the moment. He was salivating. Yow was not really in the mood for being teased and tried to wriggle behind the piano stool. Clouseau disengaged his claws from a pile of warm sweaters and Yow found himself a reluctant pianist as he was tumbled along the keys and bounced. He became a test-pilot, as he dusted the lampshades and a window-cleaner as he slid down the window-pane. Momentarily, he got the better of Clouseau as a section of his knotted tail looped a paw. Otherwise, he took a bit of a beating.

As Clouseau sat contentedly nibbling his tail Yow conceded round one and plotted revenge!

Round two was voided. Clouseau had started the chase before the official rest period was over. He insisted he only moved off his line to have a quick bite of sustenance from his bowl in the kitchen, but I suspected a sneaky attack from Yow's blind-spot and called foul!

I reckoned that overall Clouseau came out of the evenings' scrap well ahead; sure, he'd shed a few claw tips and scored a rough own-goal on his ear but had foiled cunning figure of eight knots by jumping unpredictably and doing his highly individual 'tucks and ducks'. Yow had to be helped to his drawer.

I slept well that night, undisturbed by the early spring calls from starlings. Their chattering was becoming more insistent week by week and since I had blocked their access to the porch the summer before, they had to chat each other up on either the radio aerial or the guttering.

Looking outside the sun was making a primrose appearance and I suspected that if I blinked, it might change it's mind and run for cover behind the rolls of steely cloud above.

I tapped the barometer. It read 28.5 and rising. Clouseau examined it too and pointedly suggested that it had nudged into the 'breakfast' sector. Rising meant 'more' he confided I me. Knowing we weren't going anywhere it seemed churlish not to give him a good cooked breakfast and I slung an extra egg in the pan. He enjoys an occasional treat like this.

He sat on the kitchen stool opposite me and tried to hypnotise a stray baked-bean. Looking at the assembled multitude on my plate that stared back at him, he found he couldn't concentrate and ate the loner instead.

Our breakfast was interrupted when what might best be described as a lump of wet fur bounced onto the windowsill and slid straight off.

'What the hell was that?' Clouseau asked, quite alarmed.

The wet fur came back for a second try, noticeably white this time.

'A Very Wet Cat' I replied.

The Very Wet Cat was trying to get in the window.

It probably thought it was home but in the uniformity of the snow and the obliteration of all scent marks had understandably made a mistake. It looked so thoroughly dejected that I left the warmth of the stove and gently lifted it inside.

'Whotcha do that for?'

Very Wet Cat got wetter as the snow melted and it tried

to dry itself on Clouseau. Clouseau felt that this was most inconsiderate and nudged Very Wet Cat in the direction of my trouser bottoms. The bedraggled fur finally dried to a sleek oyster and silver that could only belong to a 'she-cat'. She purred heavily in the dull glow of the fire. I noticed that Clouseau was brushing out his whiskers extravagantly.

'O. K; O.K, she can stay just a little while.'

I proffered her some egg, and this was gently dabbed up. She turned lazily to view her benefactors and warm her other flank. Facing Clouseau she made a silent meow which I certainly could not interpret. He did. He stretched up and seamlessly lowered his front paws to the floor. He paused, never taking his eyes off her. Then in a silky glide he was alongside her, mouth apart, tasting her scent.

Very Wet Cat purred in appreciation and Clouseau settled down between her and the stove. Much as he obviously found her very attractive, he still had to make certain the hierarchy of the household was not upset. In his eyes orderliness was next to Godliness and change was not to be embraced uncritically. In the light of all this, I thought that Very Wet Cat must have something rather special about her.

Later, Clouseau sat incredulous as Very Wet Cat gave birth to four kittens in his basket. He sat open-mouthed, wide-eyed and tongue-tied.

A highly communicative cat in most situations, he shut up completely. I wondered to which cat I should give a lick of sherry. Clouseau gawped. It was one thing having your basket hijacked but this turn of events was troublesome in the extreme. He looked at the huddles of fluff and the two very dark eyes in an oyster coat guarding them and

made an executive decision...he delegated the decision as to what to do to me.

He looked at me perplexed and desperate for guidance. We stared at each other staring. Behind us, a scene of natural harmony was unfolding. Very Wet Cat gently licked each kitten from toe to tip and ensured each responded properly, nuzzling-up to her and seeking sustenance. The kittens were so incredibly tiny; no longer than a packet of cigarettes. To my inexperienced eye they were indecipherable from each other, but for one, who had a white paw on the rear offside. She was quite the smallest and called for assistance with a weedy'...e..e..eeeeow' Her Mother, preoccupied with three other foragers was probably oblivious to her fourth offspring's existence. I pulled a tea-towel from the kitchen and gave her a poor imitation of a wash and wheel scrub. I called her 'Very

Little kitten' as I hadn't a proper name for her yet. The underbody hot wax could wait until 'Very Little kitten' could stand on four legs at once.

Very Wet Cat's offspring started to take more notice of their immediate surroundings after an hour or two. They couldn't as yet see, that takes five weeks or so but they'd more or less got the milk- run sorted out.

Very Wet Cat licked, tended, and slept for two days. She was obviously exhausted. Two very round black eyes kept watch and I lifted an encyclopaedia of Cat Care from the bookcase.

I thumbed in agitation through the pages:

A : Anorexia

C: Conjunctivitis

P: Pregnancy

W: Weaning...ah ha! I thought.

Very Wet Cat was still watching me intently.

A voice piped up behind me

'I know what to do!'

I turned and Clouseau had formed a warm shield around the opposite side of the basket from Very Wet Cat.

'See, it's easy, just let us get on with it, will you?'

So I did, but the following day took a day's holiday anyway. The bundles of fluff became fluffier by turn and 'Very little kitten' one got her bearings with the aid of timely nudges from Clouseau. He was clearly spellbound and took his new duties with a commitment and altruism that astonished me. After one eight- hour stint warming and protecting, he pushed open the kitchen door.

'I'm awfully stiff.'

He had a quick rummage in his bowl and before I could work out 12 Across he'd hobbled back and resumed guard. Writing the shopping list later, I added Cat Milk, Liver and Chicken, the last two just for him.

Very Wet Cat had lapped at the milk I'd warmed to 35C.; just less than the body heat of a cat. She purred an appreciative 'thanks' before crashing out once again.

Clouseau forgot his manners momentarily when he discovered the chicken.

Clouseau has a knack of sorting carrier bags into categories after I returned from a shopping trip:

Bags with Tins: may be interesting;

Bags with Packets: probably not wasting energy on;

Bags with Cellophane wrappers: Always worth a look.

As I'd dumped the Asda bags in the middle of the living- room floor, he'd carelessly kicked 'Very Little Kitten', who we'd now named 'Juno' on Dad's suggestion. 'Very Little Kitten Juno' flipped onto her back. She blinked and tried to right herself but flipped over a full 360 degrees, ending up as before. Clouseau meanwhile, had his head and shoulders in one of the carrier bags. First out of the bag was the receipt.

'The price of cigarettes... you need to quit. Apples...ugh! Don't like them!...nor peas..! Anything for me?'

'Ahaa!'

Obviously he'd found something good. A yellow tray was extracted unceremoniously by his claw-tip.

'Gottcha!'

The tray seemed not the least bit perturbed and settled itself upside down on the carpet. It really should have known better than to hang around. It received a full workout. Clouseau knew how to tone it up, since he'd practiced on the two daft dogs next door. One Two, Bat! Three

Four, Thump! The tray jumped like a bean and then as if in slow motion rotated like a windmill. It ended up back in the Asda Bag. Clouseau decided to sit it out. These bags never stayed put for long. He supposed they got bored. He could wait.

'Very Little Kitten Juno' was, meanwhile, trying to reunite herself with the basket from which she'd tumbled. I gave her a leg up and she tobogganed down the other side and bumped into Very Wet Cat who twitched one whisker in recognition and went back to sleep. So much for maternal instinct.

Cats sense movement more than sound and this is what distracted Clouseau from his Asda Bag. Very Wet Cat had stirred and lifted an oyster paw languidly into his peripheral vision.

'Hello', said Clouseau.

Very Wet Cat yawned.

'I suppose I should introduce myself formally', he said.

'Mmmmm? Very Wet Cat said.

'I'm Clouseau. I'm guarding a piece of chicken. Fancy a bit?

'Puurrhaps...'

Very Wet Cat was obviously not very impressed and Clouseau determined that she was suffering from Post Natal Feline Depression. Fancy passing up a chicken breast; no accounting for fickle female cats, he thought. He determined to knock her for six with his impersonations. He would rehearse until his act was perfect. He'd been practicing since he was a kitten and was getting pretty good. He thought his 'Chirrup' was damn good.

He was still working on his 'Injured bird impersonation'; he had to do it through clenched teeth and that was tricky, rather like being a ventriloquist. Typically, he'd seen one on the television. You might be forgiven for thinking that the T.V. is never off in my house. It is, in fact, on all day when I'm out at work, as company for Clouseau, but rarely in the evenings. Clouseau has thus had access to Richard and Judy; Pointless and an interminable number of cookery quizzes.. The advice he gives me when I'm preparing food I'm sure comes from them.

So he practiced his impersonations. Very Wet Cat seemed worth it. He'd practice on Juno, then he'd launch it on Very Wet Cat with he hoped, devastating effect. He pictured her rapt with admiration sharing a bowl of delicious, succulent, chicken wings, with him.

'Nooo.....please have some!'

'Oh , I really can't!'

'Nooo..... really do.'

'Well, no I couldn't.'

'Go on!'

'Oh alright then, if you really insist!'

He pictured her complementing him on his versatility, asking him to do more. Of course, he would bashfully decline.

Four very tiny kittens stayed close to Very Wet Cat for days and she began to take an interest in them, for which I was very much relieved. Warming milk in a saucepan every hour or so was quite tiring. Clouseau's whiskers returned to their relaxed position and he stopped swishing his tail in agitation. Should any of the kittens have been able to speak at this stage I guess they would have been pleased too since his tail had nearly knocked two of them out cold.

'How long have I got to keep this warming-lark up?' he asked.

'Only another two weeks I joked'.

His whiskers bristled before I could tell him I was only kidding.

'Tell you what I'll get the small fan heater out of the loft,' I said.

'Could I help?'

'You can watch.'

Getting into the loft requires challenging gymnastics otherwise the beams knock you out. Clouseau had been to the top of the stepladders on several occasions previously, stretching up on tiptoe to try and peer in the hatch. His balance is first class. His pink nose probed, led by his whiskers, feeling the downward of air draft as a submarine periscope would search the horizon. He couldn't quite make it up there without me, much as he would have wished.

I hadn't let him come up before as I'd been sorting it out for 10 years and never seemed to make much progress. The loft is in a constant state of flux; boxes and polythene bags everywhere. They've usually detached themselves from their label of contents. To get at anything I have first to unpack a great deal.

His new-found territory was clearly a delight. He darted about marking sack after sack with his scent glands. Occasionally, he would pause and double-check everything before with a vigorous bound he was on to a new trail.

'Clouseau, it's a heater we want, not a spider!'

'Alright, alright, but...'

Clouseau was 'on a case' and despite a bungled attempt to knit a pile of interesting wires into a winter coat he found the heater in minutes.

'It's under here by the television aerial!'

His tail tangled with the aerial on its nylon support ties. I imagine I will get Polish programmes now.

The fan heater idea was inspired and not just to warm the kittens. Clouseau would stand in front of it. His fur rippled in appreciation of the invisible masseuse.

The kittens fluffed up into tiny furry balls under the draft that circulated around Clouseau. He had a knack of getting it right and kept the direct heat off them.

When we switched it off, Clouseau had a heat perm down one flank which stood sharply to attention and looked quite ridiculous. I didn't tell him in case it hurt his feelings. Very Wet Cat might find it attractive I supposed. Spiky hair seemed all the rage these days.

The following day I had to leave them unsupervised. It was the only option. I hoped that when I got home I wouldn't be confronted by chaos.

If Clouseau had been able I'm sure that he would have had the kettle on for me, he would be so pleased to see me home.

Clouseau would have his work cut out. Undoubtedly he would have lots to tell me when I got back.

'You just won't believe the day I've had...'

Very wet cat seemed a brassy lass and was obviously of the mind that her off-spring should not be spoiled. Clouseau doted on her and them but tried not to show it. 'Very Little kitten Juno' eventually started to grow under his supervision and a special bond seemed to be created between them. Clouseau was doing pretty well given his inexperience.

After about five weeks Very Wet Cat informed me that much as she had enjoyed my hospitality, she must be heading back to her old lodgings. Very Wet Cat was, she said, concerned about squatters. She'd be back for a few nights out with Clouseau she said, and could Juno stay with him if that was o.k. since they seemed to get on so well together.

I agreed on behalf of Clouseau. He had cornered a grape under the piano and was far too busy to do any forward planning. Grapes had a wild streak and would spit juice at you unless you opted for a softly approach.

A routine re-established itself. Juno, under Clouseau's tutelage learned how to hunt the small intruders that sought safe refuge indoors. Outdoors, was out of bounds for Juno until she had had her vaccinations.

Chapter 5

Clouseau give a start. He dreamt he was in the fast lane on the motorway in the back seat of a car.

'Help, help! I've been kidnapped!' he shouted.

'Police!'

He dreamt he was miles from home with no familiar scents to protect him except the cigarette smoke. Cigarette smoke? He was indeed in the car and he was on the motorway! He watched as I stubbed the cigarette out ineffectively in the ashtray.

'Not kidnapped? So what the Hell's going on?'

'We are going to see Uncle Ron and Patch.'

A few miles went by. Juno still being very very young just snoozed on Diane's knee.

As we approached Gretna services, Dianna let Clouseau have a roam round the car. We were in the centre lane and were passing a farmer towing his horse and trailer. I caught a glimpse of Clouseau's head doing a double-take as we overtook it.

'Blimey! Ddddid...did you see that? DID you see that?!'

He strained over Diane's shoulder to get another look.

'...the size of it!'

"What's that?' I said, absent-mindedly.

'That cat-carrier on wheels!'

'What?'

'The cat-carrier you overtook!'

'Was there?'

'Yeah, the one with the thingy in the back.'

Diane interpreted.

'Clouseau, it's a horse, pet,' she said, suppressing a grin.

'A what?'

'A horse Darling; they belong in the country.' There was then silence for a couple of seconds.

Clouseau looked terrified and his eyes were black.

'No darling', she said reassuringly.

'I don't like the country at all, it's horrible!' he muttered.

He hid in the car footwell for several miles and stuck his head in an Asda bag.

'Wus', I said, teasing.

When we stopped for a coffee, Clouseau dug in his portable litter tray. The experience had clearly upset him.

'All the excitement you see', he said, apologising.

'Just don't scatter it everywhere. You can't afford to leave a trail as far as horses are concerned.'

'Stop it!' Dianna said to me, 'the wee chaps' terrified.'

'Only kidding Clouseau,' I shouted over the seat whilst he excavated for all he was worth.

He only resurfaced when we got going again.

'Has it gone?'

'Yes darling, you're safe.'

'Safe?'

'Yes, safe.'

He ventured one black eye out of the fleecy on the back seat.

' Yes, only the bulls to contend with now.' I added.

He instantly disappeared again for several minutes before re-emerging sniffing the air warily just in case. No bulls that he could see, just hundreds of little white fluffy things bouncing around in the fields. *'Sheepeses'* he exclaimed; *'Wow!'* Sheepseses, as he'd come to know them, were the pussycats of farm animals and he felt that they posed no significant threat since they were severely challenged in the intelligence department. He scrabbled up to the window and made rude gestures from behind the safety of the glass. We were exiting a roundabout at that moment and the car, used to cornering, did it well; Clouseau ended up in the footwell.

'Ouch.'

'Serves you right for being so rude', I retaliated.

He pawed the window and at least twice I caught glimpses of puzzled looks on the faces of tired drivers as a cat slid down the side window of our car. When this got too boring, Clouseau tried doing his impersonations of a nodding dog by sitting on the parcel-shelf. It must have driven the motorists following us to distraction.

Clouseau was still miming when we turned into my Dad's village. The road winds and bumps its way into this unspoilt Western side of the Lake District. Whether it was his 'Churchill Insurance' dog imitation with its slow head roll, or just the bumpiness of the road I'm not sure, but the feline-traveller wished he'd had some Dramamine.

'Ooops, sorry.'

That windy road tests everyone's stomach at times.

Uncle Ron, as Clouseau called him, always enjoyed our and his, company at weekends; Uncle Ron's cat, Patch , didn't particularly like Clouseau's visits. Whenever we arrived we always made a terrific fuss of Patch with tummy-tickles and ear-rubs, in an attempt to reassure him that we weren't the perpetrators of 'bouncings', even if we were complicit in bringing the bouncer with us. This time Patch would meet Juno for the first time.

'Hi Uncle Ron!' Clouseau was balancing on his back legs, reaching up to him.

'Hello Clouseau; want an ear scrunch?'

'Yes, but if you don't mind me asking, what's cooking?', Clouseau enquired, hoping it didn't sound too impertinent. It was of course intended as a complement to Dad's culinary expertise.

'Never you mind; you'll like it', he replied, a smile playing on his lips.

'I'd like to like it now if I may' he said, and gave Dad an ankle massage just to rub the point in.

'We'll all like it once it's cooked Clouseau.'

Clouseau went off to search out any new scents; Patch to bounce and the recipe book, just in case Dad had left it open offering a lead on the oven's contents. He was, as it were, 'on the case.'

Juno was made a great fuss of by Dad. She woke up long enough to appreciate the fuss.

Clouseau started! He must have been dreaming and nodded off on Uncle Ron's softest of soft carpet. Above him an inquisitive paw dabbed at his ear.

Clouseau wondered if Patch might just know what was for tea and so determined to be really nice to him for an hour or so and if that wasn't possible then for at least five minutes.

After thirty seconds or so this was getting very boring; after one whole minute virtually impossible. As Patch put a paw over the armchair

Clouseau gave a shoogle of his bum and blasted off, claws scrabbling at the carpet for purchase. In two bounds he was over the back of the chair. It rocked with surprise. He overshot Patch by at least a metre and hit a stack of CD's end on. They clattered off the bookcase. He failed miserably to get a grip on the polished surface and disappeared still going full tilt, following the last CD off the end.

Clouseau was a slapstick artist and you had to laugh with him. Not to do so would have been to misunderstand him and would certainly have hurt his feelings. At times he was just like a finely tuned racing car but without any brakes or intelligent suspension system.

I love practical jokers and Clouseau was a prankster. Unfortunately, rather like the wonderful comedian Tommy Cooper, the fallout from his enterprises were usually on him!

Clouseau extracted himself from the mess of CD's he'd created. They slithered and clattered a while more until he reached the security of the carpet.

'Good Boy Clouseau!'

The hint of sarcasm he'd detected in the tone of my voice stung him a little but pride took the upper hand and he walked rather stiffly out of the room. Patches' sugar mouse got a clip from his back leg on the way.

Outside he was struck by the injustice of it all. After all he'd only been going to give a Patch an affectionate bounce.

Patch, having opted to roll with the punches, if, and only if, it was wholly necessary, now tucked in tighter to the arm of the chair, his tongue gently dipping in and out of his tiny face. But for this, you would have never known that he was even ruffled. He determined to stay absolutely still for the next whole day. This was unrealistic but it was worth a try. He might succeed as he spent hours meditating about feathered foes.

Chapter 6

Patch's interest in birds had begun early in his life under the hedge where he had been born. He was from quite a large family. Somewhere he had brothers and sisters but when his parent's keepers' had moved to new employment in the city when he was only six months old he had been mistakenly left behind.

Everyone had been in the removal van at the pre-arranged time, except him. The excitement had been just a bit much for him and he'd needed to check out the hedge. When he'd returned, feeling better, the van had removed itself out of sight.

'Oh bother!' he'd said out loud. (He'd been well brought up in these first six months)

'Oh shit!' he'd said as he forgot his manners.

As I have said Patch was to become a very contemplative cat and this was the first test of his philosophical nature. Following the removal van he quickly dismissed as being unrealistic. He didn't even know where it was heading let alone how to get to that unknown place. Of course, at this stage he didn't know Clouseau so couldn't have engaged his superior powers of detection.

He'd resolved to be stoical about the whole awful business. (But he'd had a quick cry first). O.K. he'd thought, make the best of it. First, I've got a feather-lined bed, even if it is under the hedge. Second, my hunting abilities had been well proven in the last two months. He had a feather trophy for one small sparrow and a vole. He wouldn't starve. Third; he had to search hard for a third. Because you have to have three good sides to things when you're making a list like this, he'd thought long and hard. Eventually he'd found one. He could enjoy his carry-ins without them being mauled by brothers and sisters who didn't wash their paws before dinner. There was the outside chance that they might come back but he wouldn't have bet a finch's wing on it.

He'd settled down for a little nap. He was very, very good at this and spent most of the afternoon doing it.

He'd blinked; the setting sun was a watery orange and was falling rapidly down towards the sea a mere two hundred metres away. It caught his eyes and he had closed them twice, hard. He hadn't felt especially inclined to move from the snugness of his warm bed. He'd not been over-hungry and since voles and birds were at their most accessible when it got to half-light, when his vision was sharpest, he'd decided he would stay put for the time being. He'd re-arranged his Bournville-brown paws under him and faced the sun. It had caressed his whiskers and lightly tickled his chin as it sunk lower, accentuating his own rich colour. He'd luxuriated in the rich deep infra-red and thought, of absolutely nothing.

It was stiffness that had woken him. In place of the grand red orb, had been hoisted a faintly metallic and yellow one. He'd not yet been fully awake but had given a sharp 'ouch'"as a twig grazed his leg. The chill of the early morning drilled into his forepaws.

'Bbbbother.....bother, bother!' he'd said.

No-one had listened. He'd thought he'd risk an outstretched paw. Tentatively it moved forward and stretched its toes. The cold found its way in and he'd pulled it in quickly. What he'd needed was a warm breakfast and it certainly wasn't going to be found in bed unless room service miraculously appeared.

An early–bird momentarily had alighted on the hedge-top. He'd snapped into readiness but it had flown away almost immediately and he'd taken up a mantra which comforted at such frustrating moments.

'Bother, bother, rats, bother; rats.'

Well that was it then he'd thought, nothing for it but to get up, which he'd done. He'd arched his back just as far as he could, pushing higher than usual to pre-stretch his muscles. A glimmer of the Suns' back punctured the blue-grey of the horizon behind him. Right! Let's go and find breakfast, he'd thought for the second time.

That didn't prove as easy as he had imagined. He'd tried staying motionless for a half-hour under the apple tree. Two pigeons had landed ten metres up and much as he would have enjoyed one, his camouflage could not ensure his invisibility on a climb to that height. Not fancying

apples for breakfast, he'd tip-toed along the edge of the silky damp grass,

recently cut after the winter. The abandoned slivers had tickled his paws.

He'd had a wash and brush-up by rolling in an immaculate dusty border

and then on the damp grass. He'd clenched and unclenched his toes in

appreciation. Whoever provided so adequate a gentlemen's toilet must

have a well-stocked pantry and warm fire! He'd hang about and find

assorted shrubs where his feathery friends might drop in. Seeing if

anyone left a door open the house would just be a bonus.

Whilst he'd passed sometime in the shrubs, a resident robin had

chanced his wing a bit and lifted a tempting insect from within a whisker

of Patches'. Patch, oblivious, had taken the growing warmth of the

morning sun in his stride and shifted his posture to 'do' his other side.

At the back door a distinguished and white-haired gentleman had

appeared, noticed Patch and continued what he was doing. He was

making a ginger cake. Later, the aroma of home-made soup wafted out of

the kitchen window. Patch had detected a hint of beef and a few herbs.

He'd stirred his eyes in the direction of the window. Like the Bisto Kid,

he'd raised a wet nose in its' direction.

Neither his pride nor he was fully grown, and he'd pottered in the

direction of the source of the good smell, which now had invaded his senses. He'd sat and waited. Just perhaps, just maybe, the distinguished Gentleman might; just possibly..?

Patch was of a different nature to Clouseau. Clouseau would have marched in uninvited and perky; looked up at a saucepan and said *'Where's mine then?'* This little chap hadn't want to push his luck. He'd observed the treatment meted out to his maternal great-aunt in a similar situation. So he'd waited in hope.

He'd seen the man's shape behind a glass of the back door and thought that if he was patient then sometime soon the man might open the back door and take pity on him. Just maybe. The smell had made his mouth water.

He'd arranged himself cutely as the door opened and rolled onto his back.

'Mrroow'

'Hello?'

'Mrrowow'

'Well' you're in a bit of a sorry state aren't you.'

The Bourneville fur was crazed with bits of grass and a sprig of twigs was stuck to his side.

'Mrroow, ow,ow'

' Well let's see if you can be sorted out a bit,' Dad had said as he opened the door wide.

"Pleeese.'

He'd hopped over the doorstep and looked up expectantly.

'I'd like some food. Please! You see a removal truck came and

took....... Sisters...... Not back.... They went.... No food!'

Dad had understood one word of this and it was clearly expressed.

The little chap was ravenous. He also looked bedraggled and worn-out.

When a cat sits under your cooker and tries to stretch up in front of it,

pathetically clawing at the door, it usually means one thing.

'Would you like some ham?' Dad had said. It was a rhetorical

question but the answer came back instantly

'MMRROW.'

'Your talkative.'

Dad had had a ham shank the previous day and had made a stock for

soup with it. There were, however, plenty of scraps left and he'd filled a

saucer with them.

'This is great!' and he'd added a 'Thanks' for good measure and hoped

he might be offered some more. He was not disappointed and pudding,

in the form of a small tin of tuna fish was extricated from the pantry

shelf. Patch caught a glimpse inside as he nibbled a piece of ham. He'd

approved. This man could obviously hunt! It could be a good idea to

team up with him. He'd had had so little success himself. However, this man hunted; it was definitely successful but as he'd noted it couldn't be by chasing his prey since this man's legs were a bit wobbly. It must be by stealth and surprise he thought. He'd decided to hang around and see what he could learn.

His first lesson began. The gentleman stood by the glass front of a machine and with one smooth movement to open its door. Patch had peered inside. He'd ben astonished, since there perched on the shelf was a whole chicken.

'Some bird trap that', he'd said in total awe; *'Wow, you're clever!'*

He'd looked in admiration at the gentleman and silently promised him that he would sit and guard the trap all afternoon and let him know when it had caught another chicken. In return, he'd hoped for a slice of this one when it was lifted out of the trap. He'd sat on the lino working very hard for an hour. Then he'd fallen asleep, still in front of the bird trap. He'd dreamt of installing a similar trap in his hedge; he'd dreamt of a limitless supply of contraptions like this..

The door of the machine had clicked and he'd woken up.

'I guarded it every single second but I didn't see any movement..... *nothing else got caught in there'*, he'd said. *'But that one looks a good* *size.'*

As the spring sunshine had faded on the day of Patch's' first visit to my Dad, he'd felt a gentle cradle lifting of him onto the back doorstep. He'd had tried hard to explain that really he didn't mind at all sitting in front of the cooker all evening and that he'd happily work all hours there for his lodgings However it appeared that the white-haired gentleman hadn't understood. As he'd dragged his feet wearily back to the hedge he vowed he'd be back tomorrow and this time make himself indispensable.

The white-haired gentleman was an early - riser and his routine had brought him face-to-face with Patch the very next morning. As he'd opened a kitchen blind and absent-mindedly scanned the sky for weather fronts approaching or leaving this unspoilt corner of the Lake District, his gaze had been drawn to the little dark chocolate-coated creature sitting fluffed out and patiently on the coal bunker. He'd looked, the white-haired gentleman thought, even more dejected than yesterday and he must certainly be cold. A conversation I had with Dad later that day had gone a bit like this;

'Hi Dad!'

'Hello!'

'How are you?'

'Fine.'

'Good.'

'Excuse me, the phone cord is being chewed.'

'What?'

'The phone cord; he's playing with it.'

'Who is?'

'Er; Patch.'

'Er; who?'

'Patch!'

Now sometimes calls to my father could be difficult as we both have the habit of talking across each other. But this conversation took a bit of beating.

'Who's Patch?'

'The little cat who was here yesterday'.

'What little cat?'

'Oh this scruffy looking thing was hungry so I let him in and fed him.'

'Oh, you mean you've been adopted,' I'd said.

'You could put it that way; any how he's back and his playing with the phone cord.'

Dad had obviously not been too reluctant to open the door and let this stray in.

'What colour is he?' I'd asked.

'A sort of dark Bourneville chocolate.'

'Brown?'

'Yes, sort of, with a white bit on his front.'

The penny dropped.

'Is that the patch?' I'd asked.

'Well, er, yes', he'd replied.

Not only had my father befriended it but he had already given it a name. There was obviously some sort of two- way attachment.

"Would you like me to bring a basket for him?" I'd enquired.

"Oh no, he'll have to go out at night", my Dad had said.

I wondered at that time just how long that would last, since cat's have a habit of working themselves into your affections even if you don't take pity on them.

For a week Patch had been shunted with relatively complicity out of the back door at night. Presumably he didn't quite understand the reasoning behind this but had accepted it philosophically. Daytime comfort and food was worth a night under the hedge. It was warming up slowly in any case since spring had come early.

A heavy downpour at 10 o'clock as my dad opened the back door, swung the balance in Patch's' favour.

"Oh, come on, your poor beggar", my Dad had said; "but just tonight you understand". With that Patch eagerly ran back into his warm spot by the fire. Just tonight, very quickly had become just every night; Patch was more than satisfied; my Dad, I think, was secretly pleased. It seemed so unfair to turf the wee chap outside at night.

Patch had stretched out on his back; and warmed the other side of his coat.

Chapter 7

Clouseau was exploring. He wondered if Patch had a hidden horde of food anywhere. He picked up a scent but it soon petered out at a bit of chocolate crispy that appeared to have been stupid and got itself flattened under a shoe. A sorry sight, Clouseau thought. If it hadn't looked so deflated, he would have given it a run for its money. Setting off on a new trail he found some bits of fluff before his nose started to twitch involuntarily. A down current of air held the unmistakable aroma of roast sirloin. He drooled a little before elastically raising himself until the steak could be seen. It wasn't a whole one so he assumed that someone had saved it for the cats. And he was a cat wasn't he? His paw stretched out and lovingly caressed the white fat before hooking it onto the floor. It was tender and succulent. Seeming rather antisocial to eat it on the lino he carefully lifted it up and carried it to the lounge where he dropped it on the carpet.

He couldn't understand why so much fuss started. Everyone seemed to descend on him at once and his beautiful present was lifted from right under his nose.

'That's not fair! After all it was meant for me...wasn't it?'

Patch lifted an eyebrow at the commotion. Loud voices came from the kitchen.

'Would you believe it?'

'Who left the pantry door open?'

'Well, that was our supper! It'll just have to be corned beef now'.

Clouseau perked up. He liked corned beef but would have preferred the sirloin; if the steak was for supper he thought then why couldn't he have eaten it now? Sometimes there was just no accounting for human logic.

When the commotion subsided, he thought it safe to explore a little more. Everyone seemed to be ignoring him in any case. Keeping low, stomach pressed hard to the ground, he wriggled under one of the large chest-of-draws in the utility room. It was there he found an Aladdin's cave! There were several packets of chicken cat-treats and a whole paper sack that smelled delicious. It looked as if it might have a weak seam that would yield to gentle teasing by a claw. Whiskers twitching, he raised a paw

'Clouseau!!!'

Diane had caught him in the act.

He banged his head.

'*Spoilsport!*'

'Out of here right now' she said, her tone of voice leaving him in little doubt that she meant it. He learnt later that access to these supplies was exclusively my Dad's privilege. Clouseau was stung by the injustice of being born a cat.

Clouseau kept an ear and eye alert as we prepared dinner; he could distinguish between the sounds of oven doors, which usually heralded the roast things he liked and the fried things he felt were better reserved for humankind. A clicking catch suggested promising things to come.

It was Sunday morning and Dad, as usual, had been up at the crack of dawn. I had struggled up at 9 o'clock and Diane was still in bed. Whilst Dad was preparing the roast for the oven I messed about trying to look useful and greeting the cats through sleep-filled eyes.

'Morning', I said, with as much heartiness as 9 a.m. reasonably allows.

Patch raised one eyebrow and declined to comment.

Clouseau tried his very best to stand vertically and stretched till his every sinew was taut. He rubbed a wet nose into my hand.

'Breakfast please!'

'I was told you ate Patch's'", I replied.

'His? You've got to be joking; have you looked at what he eats?'

Dad kept Patch on a fairly strict regime of branded cat food; it was easiest for him and according to best Veterinary advice the dried high concentrate foods are both good for cats digestion, stay palatable longer when left out and are good at minimizing tartar on cats teeth. On one of Diane and my excursions to a vast wholesale outlet in Glasgow to buy nappies (for her sisters' triplets), we had come face to face with a monster-size sack of dried cat food with enough nutritional information printed on the reverse to pass a happy half hour. Whilst Diane had browsed among the shoes and trousers I had hauled one of these sacks on top of the tinned fruit and soup bound for Dad. The trolley had listed to port and threatened to play domino-style demolition with a rack of its brothers who lacked the benefit of a patron. I had given the trolley a tweak to the right and its equilibrium had been restored at the expense of a small torn muscle in my shoulder.

'Yes, I have seen what he eats', I said, because I bought it!' I replied, 'and I couldn't agree more with you Clouseau.'

This dry stuff seemed all the rage with the Vets and it did undoubtedly keep its flavour. It did remind me however, of the meat substitute which is served up by anaemic yet health-conscious vegetarians in their politically correct casseroles, to appeal to me. So I was with Clouseau on that one. I am puzzled by the anthropomorphism of inflicting our so-called healthy-eating on animals. The gene pool of the domesticated cat has remained more stable than that of most species for a long time. Cats must be doing most of their dietary management correctly when left to their own devices. I suppose my argument does fall down if we, as their domestic servants, don't allow them to scavenge for themselves and go outdoors mousing or whatever. As Clouseau once told me; half of the point of good food is the way it tastes, the other half is in the texture.

I opened a tin of beef and jelly. I think that Clouseau enjoyed it since he didn't lift his head until it was finished and then gave me an 'is that all?' look. It was.

I went outside and had a cigarette. Clouseau passed on that one, giving me a reproaching look. I wasn't sure if it was to do with the absence of a third spoonful or the price of fags. One cigarette costs the equivalent of one half of a tin of Whiskers.

Dad's garden always looks at its best at this time of the day when the air is clear. I never look at my best at this time whether the air is clear or not. However, I enjoy the quiet moment on a fine day.

Clouseau thanked me in the customary way of all cats after having a feed; he totally ignored all my advances to him. He strode purposively into the living room to give Patch a thorough 'bouncing'. That, I'm sure he thought would round his meal off nicely. Patch, being a few steps ahead of him, had taken the precaution of adopting a near invisible posture, tucked in very, very tight to the arm of a chair, out of Clouseau's immediate view. This he had hoped, combined with complete inertia, would ensure no surprise attacks. Patch was an unrealistic optimist.....

The morning was as fine and crystal-clear as Lakeland air can bring. From the landing window, the silhouette of Harter Fell and Muncaster Fell, three miles away, made a sharp discontinuity with the pinky-mauve of the sky. The sun was about to rise over them, diminishing these Fells from the giants they now presented. These 'outliers', guarding the central mass of Lakeland, were ancient when Roman soldiers' took their welcome warm baths at Hardknott Fort in 150 A.D. They must, like me, have felt that we are indeed part of something too special to comprehend and that mornings like this were to be 'felt', not understood. That, of course, would have depended upon whether they were on duty or not.

Clouseau, if he had been with the Garrison there, would have appreciated the comforts they had engineered. He liked to snuggle under the duvet at my Dad's on a cold morning like this. This was never appreciated by Patch, who felt quite reasonably, that the duvet belonged to him and my Dad in that order! This particular morning, Clouseau had been extracted in the process of bed-making and it had left little for him to do except stoke his furness and do his aerobics. But first he'd had to find Patch, his personal trainer!

Clouseau, as all cats, have their attention focused by objects which move and don't see inert ones very well. The survival of small rodents depends on this. Those who move usually become cat food. The only time that mice tend to move in the presence of a cat is when it becomes inevitable that the cat is going to spring. Cats, however, even in near complete darkness can detect the slightest vibrations of air from the trembling of a mouse's whiskers. Technically this should give the cats quite an advantage, if all other things were equal, but they're usually not.

Dad had the roasting-tin "organized" by 10a.m. and I made a half-hearted attempt to tame some Brussel Sprouts. The skirmish I had with them that particular morning cost me frozen finger ends and a cut which took weeks to heal. The netting bag in which the Sprouts had been trapped, became a challenge of wits after Clouseau had discovered it. It was teased from where it had been stupid enough to hang over the kitchen bench, and from there scooped into the air to test its aerodynamic qualities. It proved to him definitively that nets don't obey the laws of gravity. It swirled like a helicopter and landed squarely over Juno's tiny head with one segment slipped neatly over her erect tail. She jumped and tussled with herself and with each leap upwards enmeshed herself more securely. She crouched hard against the floor not yet sure of the nature of his assailant. It was clearly of surprising cunning, for whichever way she turned it stayed with her seeming to predict her every move. She tried his typically effective duck and tuck manoeuvre but with no effect. It now caught one of her paws and twisted around her tail. This, she thought was serious, and unfeminine since it raised her bum into an undignified position she only adopted when removed from polite company! It just wasn't cricket she thought!

The incident with the Brussel Sprout bag was only resolved after a certain amount of human intervention, grudgingly accepted by one proud, if shaken kitten. Such things would have to be watched with much more vigilance in future lest a concerted attack might immobilize her.

Clouseau sat that morning and did a full audit of all his bits. They seemed to be in the correct places but it was best to be sure in the aftermath of such a skirmish. You just never knew..... Audits were meticulous affairs beginning at his ears and migrating to each toe in turn. When all was duly accounted for, a full sort-out of his 'feathers' began using his teeth. Then, and only then, would he relax a little, settle down and have a satisfying lick, again from top to toe. This activity was completed quite vigorously just in case any scent of the assailant was to annoy him later. Sleep, in order to restore his equilibrium, he then found essential. Juno imitated his actions and found the sleeping bit easy to achieve.

It was not until coffee-time that Clouseau and Juno woke.

Patch, because of his early kitten-training, knew two aspects of life as a cat exceptionally well. The first was to conserve energy at all costs so as to be able to utilize it when required. The second was to move between two hunting or resting stations as quickly as possible since you had less chance of being detected. Patch is quite a fastidious cat. He eats modestly and carefully, never wasting a morsel. He shuns fancy stuff in foil trays decorated with the exuberant testimonials from manufacturers friends and relations.

'*Don't judge cat food by the brightness of its wrapper*', he had rather pompously instructed Dad one day. '*Go for the basic recipes. Don't buy me anything with radiant photos of happy cats devouring glistening chicken chunks!*'

His words of wisdom reminded me of a recent short break which Diane and I had had in Majorca that year. Since we had been staying in a fairly basic commercial hotel, escaping the tourist crowds and inevitable welcoming parties given by bored reps., we decided to make our evening-meal special and push the boat out. To this end we walked for miles trying to seek-out good local cooking, not lavishly advertised, nor with the ubiquitous pictures defining the number of eggs we would eat or size of the steak garnished with its price in Euros. We coined the phrase 'Pictures of your dinner café's', to indicate our feelings about these establishments. The more of them we found, the funnier the little phrase seemed. We eventually came across a super fish restaurant at the junction of two local access roads. The bright, clean and heavy cutlery, the shining glassware and the smart professionalism of its staff, formed the perfect backdrop for the delicious fresh produce. So much so that we ate there on four consecutive evenings. As we congratulated ourselves on finding a unique little place, unsullied by gordy attempts to sell itself, we turned up an adjacent side street to find a grand illuminated board. The restaurant's name shone in rosy neon lights; below it in three dimensional plastic was depicted each meal we had chosen during that week; Models of your Dinner.

In the afternoon we'd all watched a C.D. called "Cat T.V." This was a creative set of visual and audio stimuli designed to draw a cat's attention. It had hundreds of sequences depicting ping-pong balls; highly-sprung mice and rocking gerbils. For one truly remarkable half an hour Patch, Juno and Clouseau sat in perfect harmony, mesmerised by the on-screen antics and kaleidoscope of motion and sound. As the weekend evolved, an uneasy truce established itself between Clouseau and Patch. Patch continued to maintain as low a profile as was felinely possible and Clouseau amused himself by finding imaginary mice. He gave the painted flock wallpaper in the hall some detailed scrutiny, then a scent-mark or two and then a good scratch.

I considered his position as I pressed the hard skin off the top of a tin of white emulsion paint. Strange house; strange(ish) cats for company and the trauma of the journey.....I forgave him.

The French Window was a fascination to him. Since it came down to nearly ground level he could nearly touch the birds on the grass outside. This was rather tantalizing and he spent a happy Sunday morning there scaring the living daylights out of a rich assortment of feathered foes. He remarked later that it had been *'a most satisfying experience'*.

Patch, relieved of the need for constant vigilance, undoubtedly thought so too, as had a good uninterrupted nap, which tumbled comfortably on into Sunday lunchtime. Clouseau became far more interested in the kitchen from the moment the lid on the roasting-tin was removed. He, at such times, became friend to everyone and no amount of friendly discouragement would drive him away.

This Sunday, he'd sat with his eyes burning into my ear until I had taken notice. Ear-staring is a technique known only to cats and, I guess that Biologists will have, by now, isolated the gene for it. The genetic purpose might be to make other creatures feel very awkward when eating food in the cats' presence. The only escape from this intense attempt at hypnotism is, I've found, to give the cat a little of what you're having. They then feign dislike, and, only after persuasion will they eat it. The charade ensures that the cat retains its dignity and poise and that your meal goes cold. The gene is really very clever, since you then toss the ruined dinner in the cats' bowl where it is wolfed-down without a pause. Clouseau had his obligatory lick of soup from my finger and had then deftly jumped into my seat to await his seconds as I had cleared away the plates. I could almost hear him telling me to get a move-on. Seat-jumping is a technique which is probably not genetically programmed but learnt and Juno eventually got the hang of it. I can only hazard a guess from whom she had picked it up.

Whenever Clouseau was 'full', or had carefully satisfied himself that the culinary offering was not up to his high expectations, he would stride off in search of the very softest of chairs in which to sleep or sulk.

'*No, I shan't!*'

'Sorry old chap, but it's time to go'.

'Absolutely NOT!'

Clouseau wriggled valiantly against the tide of hands that were trying to push his bum into the Cat-Carrier. To ensure his safe transit out from the house to the car in darkness, cruel though it might have seemed to him at the time, we all felt it was sensible to put him in this contraption. Once in the car he usually seemed happy to be there for a while, but would soon protest.

'*You promised I wouldn't have to...*', he said, sounding hurt and defeated from behind the bars. He knew how to make you feel rotten.

'It's only for a while', I said.

'We didn't stop till Gretna last time', he replied acidly.

He had an obvious aversion to the Cat-Carrier since he associated it with going to the Vet.

Chapter 8

Juno grew steadily on her diet of Whiskers, Kittimilk and hardbits fortified with malted milk and turkey.

Week by week she was weighed-in on the kitchen scales. The scales were my Nanna's and are older than me. Juno never objected to this process. It wouldn't have really mattered if she had, since the broad copper disc of the scales nearly dwarfed her and it took very little time to perform the task adding little weights to the other side of the balance. In theory, a growing kitten can put on up to one ounce a day but she made a handsome four ounces a week which I thought wasn't bad for the runt of the litter.

Juno developed symmetrical markings; both her sides were mirror images apart from the offside white rear paw. Most striking were the two pale cream circles on her flanks. Her tail seemed attached by a pale amber ring marking the join. It looked as if it had been stuck on as an afterthought.

It was too early at nine weeks old to be sure what colour her eyes would be, but I reckoned they would turn out moss green. I thought that she was a bit cross-eyed, but no-one else seemed to notice. Her little form seemed to be pitched forward since her rear legs were two inches longer than her front giving her the appearance of a wedge. She reminded me of the cat described as LOST in the local newsagents' window:

LOST

Female Tabby Cat. Green eye; Bandaged

Left Leg; Bitten Ear; Limp. Answers to the name of Lucky.

Each day, Juno appeared more coordinated and confident. She began to pounce with unnerving accuracy at sugar-mice and squeaky balls. Anything, whether it moved or not, if it caught her attention, became fair-game. Walking across the living room carpet in socks became a game of Russian roulette. Juno would hide, wiggle and pounce, needle-like claws extended, and ambush her prey. Inanimate objects could become the focus of her attention too, for little apparent reason other than their presence in her line of sight. The vegetable rack seemed just as likely to be attacked as my feet. Sometimes, when the Television was on she would fidget back and forth in front of it, making leaps at the Lilliputian figures on the screen, only to bounce off the glass heavily. Her score for Technical Ability rated near 5 and 7; her Artistic Impression only 4 and 4!

During the day, whilst I was at work, I separated her from Clouseau, since her exuberance might have led to damage to either party.

I think that Clouseau really welcomed her company but couldn't quite figure out the need for her limb-hurling confrontations with him. I think he saw her as a bit of a delinquent. Jumping on Clouseau while he was sleeping or back-combing his tail with her sharp little teeth did not endear her to him. He called her every name in his vocabulary over the course of a few weeks. One consolation to me was that the very act of avoiding her, kept him in trim.

Another feature of her arrival had however really alarmed him, namely that his food bowl kept being inexplicably empty. This event correlated rather too well with finding Juno asleep and propped half asleep against the kitchen table hiccupping contentedly. Once he applied himself to this problem and found her half-asleep in some of his recently served tuna in jelly, he determined to get his own back. He did, of course, but all he got out of it was some junior kittibits which he found to be of a rather wishy-washy flavour. They lacked adequate seasoning and substance and so couldn't be counted as real food. The day Juno had her worming tablet sprinkled over these kittibits signalled his total disaffection with her food.

'*She eats THAT?*' he said, in total disbelief.

He had scarcely been able to control his amazement and sat there scrubbing his face and hacking! His eyes watered.

'*She's welcome to it!*' he said with lots of feeling.

When I thought about it Juno didn't like these Kittibits much either and it had taken her a couple of days with no other food to tempt her to try them. When she did, she did the feline equivalent of holding her nose, then swallowed them down fast. I told her the Vet would be very pleased.

.....

'Juno is in fine form', Victor the Vet (at our new Vets), commented as he felt the nip of her sharp front teeth on the skin of his little finger.

'Good teeth too!' I remarked.

Juno let go of the Vet's finger. She'd nipped it lightly to see if it would play. Victor was an experienced Vet. He was a modest man and needed no glossy promotional literature to advertise his competence. He was usually discovered by word of mouth. The exterior of his practice was the antithesis of the Craigpark surgery. It sat inconspicuously between Josef the Newsagent and Penny the Hairdresser (O.A.P. concessions Monday 2:30-4 p.m.) His door was decorated with an accumulation of faded cards advertising pet-grooming services; dog shampoo and conditioning (at home); equerry pedicures and lapidary. |

The door stuck as I had tried to go in, jamming my hand. A receptionist called Hailey said it had done that for years. She strapped my hand with an elastic ankle bandage. Wearing several coats of make-up, she struggled to raise heavy eyelids as I had engaged in combat with the door.

'Just give her one of these tablets every two days', Victor told me as I left. Juno didn't have her diary with her, so I made a note on her behalf. 'And what's wrong with every day?' Juno piped up.

'Give her as much food as...' Victor began.

 She piped up again.

'*Did you hear that?... as much food...*'

'...as you can get on a spoon,' Victor finished, '...four times a day'.

'*Oh drat!*' I heard Juno say distinctly.

'What about drinks?' I asked.

'*Drinks! Where?*' Juno perked up again.

'Manners!' I whispered, you're only allowed one drop of sherry a week. You'll give us all a bad name!'

'Oh, half Carnation Milk with water', said Victor.

'*Tame stuff!*' said Juno, '*Thanks a bundle!*'

She was still making cheeky comments as we got into the car.

'...and another thing', she said, 'where's my Kitten-Pack? I'm supposed to get one when I go to the Vets. They give them to all kittens. It said so on the wall.'

'I think only well-mannered kittens get them', I said.

'Well, in that case I deserved at least two.'

'Let's go and see Clouseau', I ventured.

'Let's not bother', she replied, before falling into a sulk that lasted all the way home. The phrase 'Kitten-Pack' punctuated the journey at odd intervals.

I had to give it to her, she was a gutsy kitten. She sprang into the lounge when we arrived home, her little front legs paddling at the air, in case Clouseau was waiting to bounce her. She fell flat on her face. Knocks and tumbles never bothered her and she rolled like a Jujitsu Master. Sometimes in a scrap she sought cover under Clouseau's back legs, a strategy that perplexed and confused him.

'Why did we let her stay?' Clouseau said massaging a scratched eye or nose with the back of his paw.

'Because she was a weakling', I said.

'Very funny,' he said.

The weakling exercised and started to grow quickly now. Soon she started to 'Meeow' like a proper cat. She didn't worry that the attempt often ended in a squeak. She told me that she'd work on it and practiced at all hours of the day and night.

'*Mmmeeeeeow -ow -owow*', she screeched at five one morning.

'*M —m- -m--- m ----m------ eeeeeeeeeeow!*' she stuttered.

Clouseau tried to burrow under my pillow.

After two weeks she had achieved concert pitch and might have plausibly got an audition for a cat's chorus had it not been that Clouseau bit her hard on the chin and set her confidence back.

'You realize that we'll have to go back through all that performance again Clouseau, when she gets over that nip'. I said pointedly.

'*Not if I keep biting her.*'

'Well if you do that', I said, 'it could be a case of the biter-bit when she gets bigger'.

'*Keep her on half-rations.*'

'Could there be anything in that for you?' I asked.

I needn't have bothered as sarcasm was totally lost on Clouseau.

A week later I went to the Vets for Clouseau. He needed eyedrops. Juno, in a wild attempt to escape from his bulk (He had sat on her) pummelled him with double kicks from her back paws. A nasty scratch now graced the corner of his eye and had rendered him hors de combat.

He'd run for cover among the gate legs of the kitchen table which had afforded some protection.

'*That hurt!*' he said.

I could see the gouge and I sympathized. Only a couple of days earlier Juno had caught me a playful swipe on the wrist and I was still applying Savlon.

The eye-drops worked wonders and I think that even Clouseau appreciated the soothing liquid. He normally resisted any attempt to put anything on, in, or near him.

'*We could ambush her*', he said gustily. '*I could be the decoy.*'

He was understandably irritated at her frequent attempts to comb his tail with her little teeth or attach herself to it while it was in full swish. Not only did it hurt, but you did look a bit of a twit walking around the garden with a kitten abseiling from your backside.

'What to do', I said, 'is keep your tail still at all times'. As I said this, I realized how stupid it must have sounded. Cats use their tails as humans do their facial expressions. They indicate emotion with a unique symbolism that all other cats recognize. Humans have only scratched the surface of this strange and wonderful language. We cannot begin to comprehend the subtlety of meaning attached to it. Of course we understand the basic signs; the relaxed and self-absorbed tail droop, the erect tail as we're greeted and of course the irritable swish. That's about as far as it goes.

Juno looks buoyant all the time. It's as if she expects a chicken around every corner, and even has her tail-up when I'm hoovering. This as all cat-people know is totally aberrant cat behaviour. Even when Clouseau has her by her neck, her tail's up. When he lets go, she shakes herself down, dusts herself off and comes back for more. Clouseau grudgingly admitted she had 'cattitude'.

Whilst on the telephone one evening, it dawned on me that the brief chat hadn't been punctuated by any acrobatics from Juno, who normally found the receiver cord an irresistible toy.

'Where are you eleven pence?' I shouted. Eleven pence was a pet name Diane gave to Juno as she said she was a penny short of a shilling.

'Sorry?' I heard from the other end of the line. Diane's brother-in-law and I had been chatting about St. Mirren's defeat of Celtic by three goals. Brother-in-Law has a Season Ticket for Love Street in Paisley, St. Mirrens home ground. He's one of their few supporters.

'Elevenpence, come here!' I shouted again and wished Brother-in-law a hasty goodbye.

'*What?*' Clouseau enquired from his basket. He was still half asleep.

'Go back to sleep', I told him, 'St. Mirren beat Celtic 3:0.'

'*By how many?*' he muttered.

'Three' I said.

'Great!' he said and fell back into a comfortable slumber.   .

Sometimes, unnervingly, Juno would hide and give us all a worrying time searching the house. On this occasion it was only a very quiet squeak that drew my attention to the kitchen bin. A muffled but high pitched squeak.

The squeak was covered in the sort of things which work their way down into the bottom of kitchen bins. It was having a hard time making itself heard, fighting its way through the debris of the day; several eggshells, cigarette ends, a soup-tin or three and bits of baked beans on toast that had gone a bit hard.

I had to give it credit, the squeak tried hard, but beans are acoustically dampening and eggshells simulate their synthetic counterparts which line the walls of recording studios in order to dampen echoes.

The squeak struggled upwards. Juno had no longer got her distinctive stripes and whirls but had become a kaleidoscope of vivid colours. She had been transformed into a picture; the sort that hang in galleries of modern art, the sort I call a mess. Her tail was down for once and was attempting to draw itself from the mire. A nose and whiskers appeared, followed by a chin.

'*I had an accident*', she said timorously. '*I was sort of doing a bit of bouncing about, as I do, over there by the cooker-hood, minding my own business and having a bit of a lark when...*'

'When what?' My enquiry must have seemed a little harsh to her.

'...*and I bounced a little too much*', she stuttered.

'...and?' I said, trying very hard to stifle a broad grin.

'*Well, I jumped onto this bin thing and it, well, it swallowed me up whole. I'd get rid of it. It's very, very dangerous.*' She said all this with great solemnity.

I told her that I'd think about having it neutered.

'You poor thing', I said as I took a wet tea towel and sponged what I could of the tomato sauce off her. She was squeakless throughout. When I'd finished, she made a bandy-legged stagger to the safety of her cat-igloo. She gave the bin a wary look as she passed it. Juno's bounce came from some powerful energy source deep in her genes. Her bounce was a four-paw affair and usually confused her since she inevitably landed facing the opposite way round from where she'd taken off.

One morning whilst I was shaving, she decided to inspect my bristle shaving brush.

'*Is it a baby kitten?*' she naively asked.

'No, it's a shaving brush.'

'*A what?*'

'A shaving brush is for shaving with,' I said.

Clouseau corrected me.

'*You shave with a razor, not a brush,*' he quietly reminded me.

'Yes, I put soap on with it and then I shave it off with the razor.'

'You don't shave the soap,' Clouseau corrected me again, *'You shave the stubble!'*

I glared at Clouseau. I called him a smart arse.

'I shave off the bristles,' I said with a sting in my voice, 'with the razor, after I've made them nice and soft by applying lots of soap and warm water with the bristle brush,' I said pointedly at Clouseau. 'That good enough for you?

'You're getting better,' was all he said in reply.

I made a mock lunge at him with the razor and he obviously thought the better of making any cheekier comments since he disappeared down the stairs. I heard him say something about me having no sense of humour in the morning. He was, of course, absolutely right.

'Now Juno,' I said, 'if you could just move over there a little bit.' I reached for the soap.

Juno didn't move sideways. She jumped, bounced and bounced again. Her jump placed her on the soap. Her first bounce took her onto the toilet rolls, which cushioned her fall and her second bounce over the toilet seat and inelegantly into the bowl. The lid had been up.

In the mirror I watched as her front paws slipped off the seat and her back paws landed in the bowl. She tried to defy gravity by lunging at the seat with one paw. This turned out to be a mistake since if she had stayed perfectly still, she could have prevented what followed. Her seven-inch form extended to ten in what was now a futile attempt to keep an anchor on the seat. Her back paws hit the water and panicked, throwing her into a half-tuck; this in turn flipped her upside down her head completely under water, whiskers first.

'Oh hell!' I swore as I cut my chin. I grabbed at her back legs which were threatening to follow her front ones round the U- Bend.

Her position reminded me of one I'd assumed years before as I'd stretched myself along the bulk of an outboard motor in the middle of Loch Fyne on a stormy afternoon. I had been trying to change a propeller pin. As the boat rocked rhythmically I had taken several emersions head first in the icy water.

Juno made a defiant swipe at the seat as I brought her to safety. 'That,' I said, brandishing a towel, 'is what comes of disturbing a man whilst he's shaving!'

She gave me a wet, cross-eyed blink and sneezed hard.

She walked stiffly through the lounge for the second time in two weeks.

'*When can I go out?*" she said abruptly as I came down the stairs.

'What?' I said absent-mindedly picking up the newspaper from the doormat.

'*Outside, to scare things.*' Juno always got straight to the point.

'Not until you've had your next innoculation from the Vet," I replied.

There was a pause. Her previous visit had been sullied by the failure of a 'Kitten-Pack' to materialize, so understandably she was torn between the prospect of getting one on the next visit and being short-changed a second time.

'*Perhaps*,' she said with quiet reasonability, '*if you were to ring in advance and order a Kitten Pack before we went, then they would be sure to have it ready.*'

I considered it unfair not to disappoint her and so rang the Vet that same day. He told me that he would see her and that they did have some Kitten-Packs left. I felt like a scrounger. 'Kitten-Pack awaiting!' I shouted to Juno.

Her delight, as she was presented with it, was expressed by the vigorous rubbing of the sides of her mouth along all its sides. It contained in order of importance, (written in three languages); A large pack of Chicken and Rice Mouse Shapes (prepared with succulent shredded chicken breast); a 55-page kitten handbook. (Holding the promise of being rippable and rustly); a plastic blue wheel with a pink mouse trapped inside. (Juno commented that she considered the mouse must have been stupid to get itself in there in the first place) and a woolly ball (smelling deliciously of Cat-Nip).

Juno had been as effusive in her thanks to the receptionist as the receptionist had been altruistic. 'No, have two Kitten-Packs,' she had said to me. 'What a very fine little kitten!'

'Are you sure?' I'd said hopefully, on Juno's behalf.

'Of course!'

Juno, during this exchange, was, all the time attempting to look just as small, cute and kitten-like as possible.

'*I like it there,*' she confessed to me on the way home.

'How was the inoculation?' I said to her.

'*What innoculation?*'

She purred contentedly all the way home.

Chapter 9

Clouseau tried to do his best to look really absorbed with one of the woolly balls which Juno had given to him in a moment of selflessness. He even gave it a cursory bat with his paw just to show her how much he appreciated it. When you've got a pure wool rug; a Marino woollen jumper (even with a hole in its sleeve); two Pringle jumpers and a hand-knitted scarf, woolly balls tend though, however hard you try, to pale into insignificance. Even so, her altruism had touched him slightly and he felt that, given time if more presents were offered, he might actually learn to tolerate Juno.

After tiring of her mice-in-wheels Juno graduated to the pleasures of observing the one-and-a-half-hour washing machine cycle. She took up this new hobby after chasing the tassel on my jacket through the washing machine's open door.

'Out!' I'd said sternly.

'*What?*' came the cheeky reply.

'Out now! Otherwise you'll be a furball in seconds.'

She looked undecided and plainly didn't understand what I was talking about. I relieved her of her prize tassel and put her on the kitchen bench where I could talk to her Man to Woman.

'Look, little one,' I said evenly, 'washing machines, hoovers and cats are sworn enemies and their animosity (she was good at languages), goes back to their first co-residence in the domestic environment sixty years ago. Most cats have by now incorporated this enmity into their genes and so don't need to be told. You obviously haven't, so I'm telling you.'

'*Wouldn't an attempt at reconciliation on my part help?*' she enquired querulously.

'No,' I said, and was lost for more words than this. Clouseau came to my rescue.

'*It's because,*' he said with utmost seriousness, '*they hunt in packs; sometimes they even get an electric mixer as an ally. When they all get going at the same time it takes an exceptionally brave cat to go into any kitchen. There is only one domestic appliance that you can really trust and that is the cooker. It's always nice and quiet and; if you treat it with great respect can become a kitten's best friend. It's always cosy and warm and it never bothers cats unless they are silly enough to jump on its head. Then, they will sting you.*'

'Thank you Clouseau,' I said. His intervention had been well timed. I hoped that his explanation might persuade her to give the interior of the washing machine a wide berth.

Only a few days later I realized that she hadn't remembered his advice. A small face poked itself into the mixer-bowl whilst the mixer was switched on to a cycle that was termed "intermittent". She told me that she just had wanted to try a bit of the creamy looking mixture. She found out by way of reward that these contraptions spit at you and decorate your fur extravagantly.

Little incidents such as these, Juno philosophically regarded as part of the rich tapestry of life. They were even to be savoured as enriching experiences that fortified her character. (She didn't quite put it this way). She was however becoming the sort of cat who shrugged her shoulders and got on with life.

As I was thinking about this, she made an effort to jump into the front of the T.V. set. She was obviously totally unaware that the front was solid glass. She hit it head on and fell back with a little squeak into Clouseau's basket situated in front of it. He, as primo catte, had a complementary ticket to the television Dress Circle. Juno shook her head and repeated the manoeuvre, this time trying harder and taking a longer run at it. Bouncing spectacularly off it, she landed on her back; squeaked twice this time, and added television-sets to the list of items which should best be approached with a degree of caution.

Clouseau had been six months older than Juno when we adopted him so though still very inquisitive he wasn't quite as intrigued by everything around him as this little one was. Clouseau had encountered some 'things' before. Carpets, for instance, he knew very well were for the sole purpose of scratching whilst books, quite definitely, were for sitting upon. Juno was not at all certain if books were for eating or shredding so she would try anything that came to mind until told otherwise. She did understand that ash-trays were for tipping over. Clouseau had told her this, having overheard me talking of the importance of emptying them. Juno thought, I suppose, that she was helping me to tidy-up. She took me aside once and told me that she didn't really approve of smoking. She was however fascinated by the wisps of smoke which drifted off the end of cigarettes, frequently launching herself at them, puzzled by their lack of substance.

We played with soap bubbles too, the sort that come out of a tubs, the sort with small rings on sticks inside their lid. The kaleidoscope of dissolving oily spheres left her bemused. They would wobble, drift and burst just as her whiskers grazed their surface, peppering her in molecular-sized droplets. Their behaviour was enigmatic and frustrating. Sometimes they would herd like frogspawn and shiver on the carpet for a second or two before popping.

I understood a little about surface tension in liquid spheres but I couldn't have explained their formation to her. I've always thought that the measure of understanding anything is if you can explain it to someone else. I could not have explained their behaviour to Juno. She proved my inadequacy in respect of this, most days of the week.

Chapter 10

'What's that?' Juno once said abruptly.

'What's what?'

'That white thing up there!'

'The moon,' I'd replied.

'The MOOooon; the Moooon.' She repeated the word and massaged it a bit giving it a heavy accentuation. *'What's a Moooooon?'*

'It's like the Earth except no one lives there.' It was an abrupt and rather unhelpful explanation but I thought it might do.

"Oh!"

She did ask me if we could get a closer look and I told her that that wouldn't be possible tonight. I said that if we got closer than it would be just like a very big round ball.

'Then why doesn't it fall down? she'd said.

I should have anticipated that question (for which I had no answer) and not made any reference to balls. She chased balls and they invariably came down unless they got themselves foolishly stuck behind furniture.

I left her staring at the 'MOOoon' from the kitchen window. For all I knew, she might have figured out how to calculate 3D geometry and have been working on a trajectory to get a closer look at this new novelty.

Slung over my shoulder, one or both of the cats would come out to the end of the garden on a fine night, and have a contemplative moment with me. Juno's attention span didn't match Clouseau's as yet, since she was only a kitten; she would begin to figit and return to the warm wool rug by the fire. On one rare occasion we were all entertained by a whimsical display of the Northern Lights. The questions I was asked about these dancers in the sky would have been enough to task Einstein.

If you enjoyed this unashamedly anthropomorphic tale then you might like *Juno's Bedtime story'* soon to be published.

Thank you for reading *For the Love of Cats.*

Christopher J. F. Gibson

Printed in Poland
by Amazon Fulfillment
Poland Sp. z o.o., Wrocław